Phillips Brooks

Phillips Brooks's Poems

Phillips Brooks

Phillips Brooks's Poems

ISBN/EAN: 9783337386726

Printed in Europe, USA, Canada, Australia, Japan

Cover: Foto ©Andreas Hilbeck / pixelio.de

More available books at **www.hansebooks.com**

Phillips Brooks's Poems.

Soothing them in sorrow,
Arming them in strife,
Opening wide the tombdoors
Leading into life.

London.
Ernest Nister
24 St. Bride Street E.C.

Printed by E Nister, at Nuremberg
(Bavaria.)

New York:
E. P. Dutton & Co.
31 West Twenty Third Street.

And they came with haste, and found Mary and Joseph, and the Babe lying in a manger.

O Little Town of Bethlehem

 little town of Bethlehem,

How still we see thee lie;

Above thy deep and dreamless sleep

The silent stars go by.

Yet in the dark streets shineth

The everlasting light;

The hopes and fears of all the years

Are met in thee to-night.

 nd there were in the same country shepherds abiding
in the field, keeping watch over their flock by night.

morning stars together

Proclaim the holy birth,

And praises sing to God the King,

And peace to men on earth.

or Christ is born of Mary,

And gathered all above,

While mortals sleep the angels keep

The watch of wondering love.

Unto you is born this day in the city of David a
Saviour, which is Christ the Lord.

How silently, how silently,

The wondrous gift is given,

So God imparts to human hearts

The Blessings of His Heaven.

o ear may hear His coming,

But in this world of sin,

Where meek souls will receive Him still,

The dear Christ enters in.

Where Charity stands watching,

And Faith holds wide the door,

The dark night wakes; the glory breaks,

And Christmas comes once more.

Oh Bless our God, ye people, and make the voice
of His praise to be heard.

 Holy Child of Bethlehem,

Descend to us we pray,

Cast out our sin and enter in;

Be born in us to-day.

We hear the Christmas angels

The great glad tidings tell;

O come to us, abide with us;

Our Lord Emmanuel.

The Voice of the Christ Child.

The earth has grown cold

with its burden of care,

But at Christmas it always is young,

The heart of the jewel burns lustrous and fair,

And its soul full of music breaks forth on the air,

When the song of the Angels is sung.

The feet of the Christ-child
fall gentle and white.

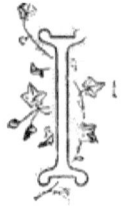It is coming, old earth, it is coming to-night,

On the snowflakes which cover thy sod,

The feet of the Christ-child fall gently and white,

And the voice of the Christ-child tells out with delight

That mankind are the children of God.

He giveth snow like wool.

On the sad and the lonely, the wretched and poor

That voice of the Christ-child shall fall;

And to every blind wanderer opens the door

Of a hope which he dared not to dream of before,

With a sunshine of welcome for all.

The feet of the humblest may walk in the field

Where the feet of the holiest have trod,

This, this is the marvel to mortals revealed,

When the silvery trumpets of Christmas have pealed,

That mankind are the children of God.

While the earth remaineth, seed-time and harvest, and cold and heat, and summer and winter, and day and night shall not cease.

CHRISTMAS ONCE IS CHRISTMAS STILL.

The silent skies are full of speech,

For who hath ears to hear;

The winds are whispering each to each,

The moon is calling to the beach,

And stars their sacred mission teach

Of Faith, and Love, and Fear.

But once the sky its silence broke,

And song o'erflowed the earth,

The midnight air with glory shook,

And angels mortal language spoke,

When God our human nature took

In Christ the Saviour's birth.

nd Christmas once is Christmas still;

    The gates through which He came,

And forests wild and murmuring rill,

And fruitful field and breezy hill,

And all that else the wide world fill

Are vocal with His name.

Shall we not listen while they sing

    This latest Christmas morn,

And music hear in everything,

And faithful lives in tribute bring

To the great song which greets the King

Who comes when Christ is born.

Constant Christmas.

The sky can still remember
    The earliest Christmas morn
When in the cold December
    The Saviour Christ was born.

And still in darkness clouded
    And still in noonday light,
It feels its far depths crowded
    With Angels fair and bright.

never fading splendour!

O never silent song!

Still keep the green earth tender,

Still keep the gray earth strong;

Still keep the brave earth dreaming

Of deeds that shall be done,

While children's lives come streaming

Like sunbeams from the sun.

No star unfolds its glory,

No trumpet's wind is blown,

But tells the Christmas story

In music of its own.

Still keep the green earth tender,
Still keep the grey earth strong.

No eager strife of mortals

In busy field or town

But sees the open portals

Through which the Christ came down.

O Angels sweet and splendid,

Throng in our hearts and sing

The wonders which attended

The coming of the King.

Till we, too, boldly pressing

Where once the Angels trod

Climb Bethlehem's Hill of Blessing,

And find the Son of God.

A Christmas Carol.

Everywhere, everywhere, Christmas
          to-night!
Christmas in lands of the fir-tree
          and pine,
Christmas in lands of the palm-tree
          and vine,
Christmas where snow-peaks stand
          solemn and white,
Christmas where corn-fields lie
          sunny and bright.
Everywhere, everywhere,
          Christmas to-night!

Christmas where children are hopeful and gay,

Christmas where old men are patient and gray,

Christmas where peace, like a dove in its flight,

Broods o'er brave men in the thick of the fight

  Everywhere, everywhere, Christmas to-night!

For the Christ-child who comes is the Master of all.

No palace too great and no cottage too small,

The angels who welcome Him sing from the height,

"In the City of David a King in His might."

  Everywhere, everywhere, Christmas to-night!

Where snow-peaks stand solemn and white.

Then let every heart keep its Christmas within,

Christ's pity for sorrow, Christ's hatred of sin,

Christ's care for the weakest, Christ's courage for right,

Christ's dread of the darkness, Christ's love of the light

   Everywhere, everywhere, Christmas to-night.

So the stars of the midnight which compass us round

Shall see a strange glory, and hear a sweet sound,

And cry "Look! the earth is aflame with delight,

O sons of the morning, rejoice at the sight."

   Everywhere, everywhere, Christmas to-night

He leadeth me

beside

the still waters.

An Easter Carol.

Tomb, thou shalt not hold Him longer;

Death is strong, but Life is stronger,

Stronger than the dark, the light,

Stronger than the wrong, the right,

Faith and Hope triumphant say

Christ will rise on Easter Day.

While the patient earth lies waking

Till the morning shall be breaking,

Shuddering 'neath the burden dread

Of her Master, cold and dead—

Mark! she hears the Angels say

Christ will rise on Easter Day.

Up and down our lives obedient

Walk, dear Christ, with footsteps radiant,

Till those garden lives shall be

Fair with duties done for Thee;

And our thankful spirits say,

Christ arose on Easter Day.

For lo!
the winter is past.
the rain is over
and gone.

And when sunrise smites the mountains,

Pouring light from Heavenly fountains,

Then the earth blooms out to greet

Once again the blessed feet;

And her countless voices say

Christ has risen on Easter Day.

I know that my Redeemer liveth.

Easter Angels.

God hath sent His angels

To the earth again,

Bringing joyful tidings

To the sons of men.

They who first at Christmas

Thronged the Heavenly way,

Now beside the tomb-door

Sit on Easter Day.

 ngels sing His triumph

As you sang His birth,

"Christ the Lord is risen,

Peace, goodwill on earth."

In the dreadful desert,

Where the Lord was tried,

There the faithful angels

Gathered at His side.

He shall give His angels charge over thee, to keep thee in all thy ways.

nd when in the Garden,

Grief, and pain, and care

Bowed Him down with anguish,

They were with Him there.

Yet the Christ they honour

Is the same Christ still,

Who, in light and darkness,

Did His Father's will.

The flowers appear on the earth; the time of the singing of birds is come.

And the tomb deserted

Shineth like the sky,

Since He passed out from it

Into Victory.

God has still His angels

Helping at His word

All His faithful children,

Like their faithful Lord.

As a bird that wandereth from her
nest, so is a man that wandereth from
his place.

Soothing them in sorrow,
　　Arming them in strife,
　Opening wide the tomb-doors,
　　Leading into life.

Father, send Thine angels
　　Unto us, we pray,
Leave us not to wander
　　All alone our way.

Let them guard and guide us,
 Wheresoe'er we be,
Till our resurrection
 Brings us home to Thee.

What shall I render

     unto the Lord

  for all His benefits toward me?

Ps. cxvi. 12.

www.ingramcontent.com/pod-product-compliance
Lightning Source LLC
Chambersburg PA
CBHW032141270626
47172CB00009B/843